POWER RANGERS JUNGLE FURY

FANGS AND FURY

Adapted by Slade Stone from the original script by Jackie Marchand
Illustrated by Scott Neely and Candace Schinzler-Bell

TM and © BVS Entertainment, Inc. and BVS International N.V. All rights reserved.

Dalmatian Press, LLC 2008. All rights reserved. Printed in the U.S.A.
The DALMATIAN PRESS name and logo are trademarks of Dalmatian Press, LLC, Franklin, Tennessee 37067.

09 10 11   NGS 33946 10 9 8 7 6 5 4 3 2
17423 Power Rangers 8x8 - Jungle Fury: Fangs and Fury

On a mountaintop near Ocean Bluff a temple looms. Here rules Dai Shi—an ancient, dark-hearted mastermind who has been released back into the world. With his Rin Shi warriors and monstrous allies, he seeks to retake the planet and destroy all human life.

Only one thing stands in his way...

The Jungle Fury Power Rangers! Trained at the Kung Fu School by the Master of the Pai Zhuq—the Order of the Claw—these three skilled teens channel their animal spirits to battle the forces of evil.

Casey channels the Red Tiger. As the Red Ranger, he leads his team, though it takes all three working as one to defeat their foe.
Theo, the Blue Ranger, channels the clever Blue Jaguar.
Lily, the Yellow Ranger, calls on the swift-footed Yellow Cheetah.
Together they form a united force of fury!

In the shadows of Dai Shi's temple, five mysterious creatures stand before their master. They are an elite squad of venomous warriors, each with a unique and treacherous poison.

Rin Shi Cobra—cold-blooded and lethal.

Rin Shi Centipede—who can strike a hundred times before a foe can respond.

Rin Shi Scorpion—
with a hypnotic
dance and a sting
finish.
Rin Shi Gecko—
cunning and swift.
Rin Shi Toad—
slow but strong,
with poisonous
warts to ward off
attacks.

"You will be my Five Fingers of Poison. Go and spread fear from the highest rooftop," commands Dai Shi. "That will take my power to the next level, in preparation for The Arrival!"

The five warriors bow—then slither and scuttle off in obedience.

In his throne room, Dai Shi hears the screams and begins to glow with energy. He gathers more and more power until he gives a triumphant roar!

And in the Jungle Karma Pizza Parlor, three teens hear the screams and grab their Solar Morphers—with a cry of:

Jungle Beast, Spirit Unleashed

"With the strength of a Tiger!" calls Casey. "Jungle Fury Red Ranger!"
"With the speed of a Cheetah!" calls Lily. "Jungle Fury Yellow Ranger!"
"With the stealth of a Jaguar!" calls Theo. "Jungle Fury Blue Ranger!"
"We summon the animal spirits from within. Power Rangers, Jungle Fury!"

The valiant three confront the villainous five in a test of skill and smarts.
"Surprise!" calls the Red Ranger. "We're here to stop you."
"Think again!" jabs the Scorpion. "So, you are the Pai Zhuq students."
"I'm not impresssssesed," says the Cobra.
"They look pretty sorry to me," snaps the Gecko.
"And ugly," adds the Toad.
"Let's get this fight started!" declares the Centipede.

With a horrible roar, the warriors cry:
By the power of the Dai Shi—inner beasts, arise!
The three power Rangers watch in amazement as the creepy creatures transform into the Five Fingers of Poison!
"A hundred legs to strike you—I am Rantipede!"
"Fangs full of venom—I am Naja!"

Rantipede charges the Blue Ranger and lands a flurry of punches.

"Whoa!" says the Yellow Ranger. "And they say *I* have fast hands!"—but her attention quickly goes to Stingerella, as the two dance around each other.

The Red Ranger delivers a blow to Toady, but is repelled. "Yow!" he exclaims. "That's one tough toad! It's time to combine with our animal spirits!"

"Three spirits—work as one!" call the three.

"Jungle Fury Power Rangers!"

Their cat spirits spring into the action to pit claw against stinger, fang against fang. But before Casey can leap into his Tiger Zord, Naja strikes and delivers a poisonous bite.

"Oh, no!" cries Lily, as she watches the Red Ranger fall to the ground.

"Hang in there, man!" cries Theo.

"Sssssssoon the end will come," taunts Naja. "But, look! Here is the sssssserum—the antidote. Do you risssssk going for it?"

"We—we gotta try," moans Casey. "Come on, team. We can't let them win."

With his last ounce of strength, Casey calls with his teammates:

JUNGLE PRIDE MEGAZORD!

The great cat spirits form the huge Magazord—
armed and angered!

Rantipede delivers strikes. Naja swipes with two
sharp blades. Gakko hurls projectiles. Stingerella
whirls, dodges, and stings. Toady tosses an
exploding ball—and the Megazord begins to stagger!

"We may be down..." says Lily.

"But we're not out!" calls Theo.

The Rangers give a battle cry and the Megazord leaps toward the monsters. It begins to spin with speed and power!

"Care to take a spin?" calls Lily as Stingerella is sent flying.

Gaining velocity, the Jungle Pride Megazord takes out all Five Fingers of Poison with the Savage Spin. As the creatures fall to the ground, the Megazord grabs the vial of antidote.

From far off in his temple, Dai Shi
feels the pang of defeat.
"No!" he roars.

"You got lucky thissssss day," snarls the Cobra, as the five fiends retreat.

"Luck had nothing to do with it," says Casey, as the three friends regroup. "Heart, brains, and teamwork triumph over terror—any day."